ot long ago, beneath the wall of a beautiful

old opera house, there lived a little bee. Her

home was a garden full of flowers. This garden

was also home to many other clever little bugs

that could do all sorts of wonderful things.

Every night, just as the sun would set, the bugs would rest from their play in the garden and would gather at the grate beneath the opera house wall. If they listened carefully, they could hear voices singing and instruments playing the most beautiful music imaginable.

The little bee would quietly take her place on top of a toadstool to listen beside the other bugs. Some nights, she would close her eyes and imagine that it was she, singing on the stage in the opera house. The little bee could hum quite well, but had never tried to sing, because she was very shy.

She was not like the spider, who

spun wonderful, silky webs . . .

. . . Or, like the grasshopper who was so brave that he could jump from rock to rock without being afraid.

One warm summer evening, the bugs once again finished their chores and sat down at the grate to listen. They waited, and listened... then listened, and waited, but there were no sounds of instruments tuning; no one began to sing. The opera had been cancelled!! The bugs were quite upset, and chirped among themselves in disappointment.

About that time, the little bee had a thought. It was a very scary thought!! What if she were to sing instead? If she did, would the bugs stay and listen? How would she know if she did not try?

At first the hum she made was quite like a squeak! But then, she took a deep breath and tried again. This time, her hum was soft and sweet. As she kept humming, her courage grew and suddenly . . .

. . . she was all but buzzing a beautiful aria that was a garden favorite! The bugs were surprised, but they did not walk away. They were very happy! The opera was not cancelled after all. They each made themselves comfortable around the grate and listened to the opera bee's first performance. It would be the first of many more to come!!